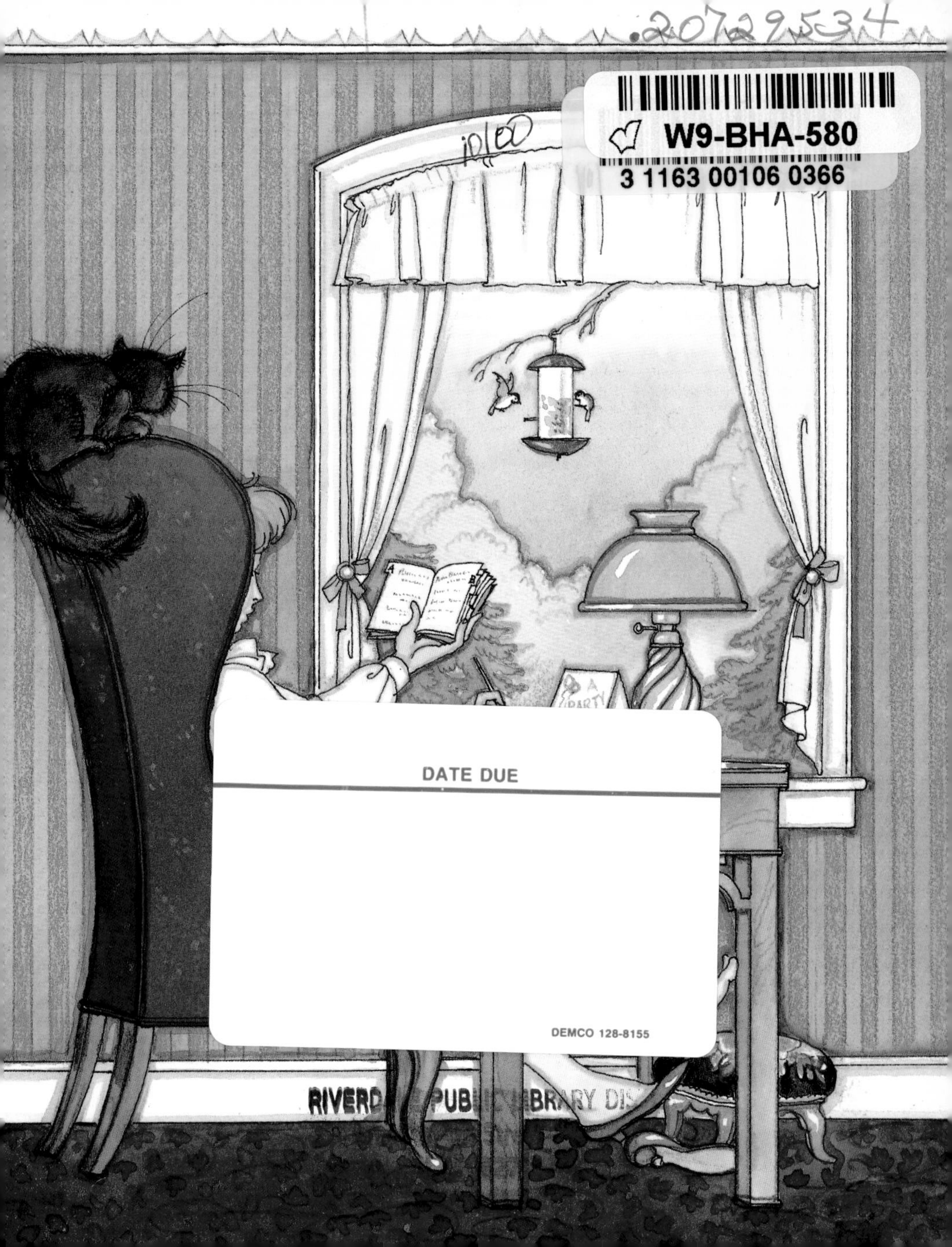

HAPPY BIRTHDAY

RIVERDALE PUBLIC LIBRARY DISTRICT
208 West 144th Street
Riverdale, IL 60827-2788
Phone: (708) 841-3311

RIVERDALE PUBLIC LIBRARY DISTRICT

HAPPY BIRTHDAY

Poems selected by
LEE BENNETT HOPKINS
Illustrated by
HILARY KNIGHT

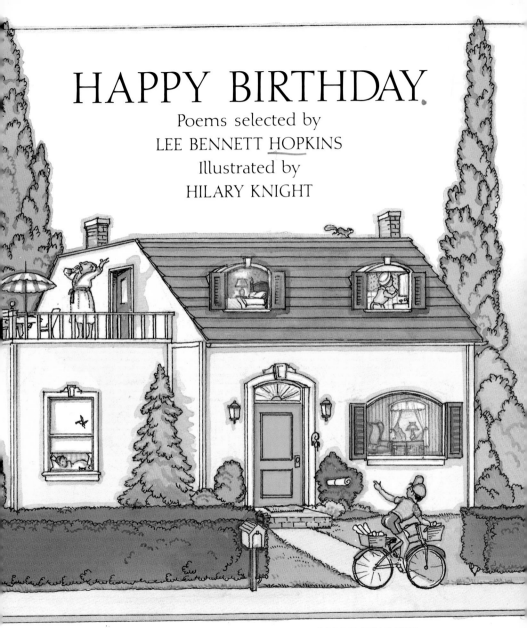

SIMON & SCHUSTER BOOKS FOR YOUNG READERS
Published by Simon & Schuster
New York · London · Toronto · Sydney · Tokyo · Singapore

✓I. Title ✓1. Birthdays -- Poetry.

For "Royal Dude"
Born: April 22, 1989
L . B . H .

To Trina for "Ruffey"
Born: January 1, 1978
H . K .

A Special Day

Today the sky
Is bluer than ever.
Today the birds
will sing forever.
Today I'll shout
and blow my horn.
Today is the day
that I was born!

Sandra Liatsos

from
A Bunch of Poems and Verses

How old will you be on your birthday?
four?
five?
six?
seven?
eight?
nine?
ten?
Whatever you are on your birthday
you
were
never
that
old
before,
you
will
never
be
that
young
again.

Beatrice Schenk de Regniers

My First Birthday Gift

They didn't give me
a doll, or book,
a stuffed giraffe
or game.
On the day I was born
my present
was my name!

Sandra Liatsos

from
Happy Birthday to You!

Today you are you! That is truer than true!
There is no one alive who is you-er than you!
Shout loud, "I am lucky to be what I am!
Thank goodness I'm not just a clam or a ham
Or a dusty old jar of sour gooseberry jam!
I am what I am! That's a great thing to be!
If I say so myself, HAPPY BIRTHDAY TO ME!"

Dr. Seuss

Birthday Surprise

My birthday came, and in a box
That I got from my brother,
I found another little box,
And in THAT box, another.
And there inside the smallest one—
Oh, hurry, hurry, HURRY—
I found a little baby mouse,
All soft and warm and furry.

Margaret Hillert

Birthday Cake

If little mice have birthdays
(and I suppose they do)

And have a family party
(and guests invited too)

And have a cake with candles
(it would be rather small)

I bet that birthday CHEESE cake
would please them most of all.

Aileen Fisher

Invitation

My birthday invitation
has balloons
of red and blue.

It says *come soon*
and *please reply,*

My name is on it too.

It tells the place where we will meet
And shows the time and date.

So *please reply*
And say you'll *come*

to help me celebrate!

Myra Cohn Livingston

On This Birthday of Yours

On this birthday of yours
The other days of the year
Whimper and whine
Shedding tear after tear:

"What a *marvelous* hubbub!
What a *fabulous* fuss!
We wish all this hoopla
Could be happening to us!"

Beverly McLoughland

Pinning the Tail on the Donkey

Pinning the tail
on
the
donkey

is a
game
that's
as fun
as can
be

except
for the time
Charlotte
got all mixed up

and started to pin it on *me*!

Myra Cohn Livingston

Birthday

The next best thing to Christmas,
the next best day to prize
is a birthday, when you're special
in everybody's eyes.

The next best thing to Christmas
if it's summer, spring, or fall,
is a birthday with a party
and a birthday cake and all.

Aileen Fisher

The Nicest Part

Paper hats and frosted cakes;
Favors that my mother makes.
Presents wrapped and tied with bows;
Guests all dressed in party clothes.
Candles glowing warm and bright
Shedding such a pretty light.
Laughter, whispers, then a shout—
Time to blow the candles out!
I make a wish for me and you
And hope the birthday wish comes true.
The nicest part of birthday fun
Is *sharing* it with everyone!

Jean Conder Soule

Birthday, Birthday, Birthday

Balloons on the ceiling
Balloons on the floor

Hoppy-poppy birthday
Hoppy-pop some more.

Candles on the big cake
Candles on the floor

Huffy-puffy birthday
Huffy-puff some more.

Icing on my fingers
Icing on the floor

Sticky-licky birthday
Sticky-lick some more.

Ice cream on my new shirt
Ice cream on the floor

Slippy-drippy birthday
Slippy-drip some more.

Presents on the table
Presents on the floor

Happy-snappy birthday
Happy-snap some more.

Nancy White Carlstrom

The Birthday Child

Everything's been different
   All the day long,
Lovely things have happened,
   Nothing has gone wrong.

Nobody has scolded me,
   Everyone has smiled.
Isn't it delicious
   To be a birthday child?

Rose Fyleman

Birthday

A birthday is a special thing
With cards and gifts and songs to sing;
A cake with candles all about
And wishes when you blow them out;
And one more year of standing tall
To add a mark upon the wall;
A day of extra special fun
To dream about when it is done.

Margaret Hillert

The Wish

Each birthday wish
I've ever made
Really does come true,
Each year I wish
I'll grow some more
And every year

I

    DO!

A. Friday

A star danced
and under that
was I born.

William Shakespeare

The End

ACKNOWLEDGMENTS

Thanks are due to the following for works reprinted herein:

Aileen Fisher for "Birthday Cake" from *Runny Days, Sunny Days* (Abelard-Schuman, 1958). Copyright renewed by Aileen Fisher. Used by permission of the author, who controls all rights.

HarperCollins, Inc., for "Birthday" from *In One Door and Out the Other* by Aileen Fisher (Crowell). Copyright © 1969 by Aileen Fisher. Used by permission of HarperCollins, Inc.

Margaret Hillert for "Birthday" and "Birthday Surprise." Used by permission of the author, who controls all rights.

Sandra Liatsos for "A Special Day" and "My First Birthday Gift." Used by permission of the author who controls all rights.

Macmillan Publishing Company for "Birthday, Birthday, Birthday" from *Graham Cracker Animals 1-2-3* by Nancy White Carlstrom. Text Copyright © 1969 by Nancy White Carlstrom. Reprinted by permission of Macmillan, Inc.

Beverly McLoughland for "On This Birthday of Yours." Used by permission of the author, who controls all rights.

Excerpt from *Happy Birthday to You* by Dr. Seuss. Copyright © 1959 by Theodor S. Geisel and Audrey S. Geisel. Copyright renewed 1987 by Theodor S. Geisel and Audrey S. Geisel. Reprinted by permission of Random House, Inc.

The Society of Authors for "The Birthday Child" by Rose Fyleman. Reprinted by permission of The Society of Authors as the literary representative of the Estate of Rose Fyleman.

Jean Conder Soule for "The Nicest Part." Used by permission of the author, who controls all rights.

Marian Reiner for the selection from *A Bunch of Poems and Verses* by Beatrice Schenk de Regniers. Copyright © 1977 by Beatrice Schenk de Regniers; "Pinning the Tail on the Donkey" and "Invitation" from *Birthday Poems* by Myra Cohn Livingston (Holiday House, New York). Copyright © 1989 by Myra Cohn Livingston. All reprinted by Marian Reiner for the authors.

SIMON & SCHUSTER BOOKS FOR YOUNG READERS, Simon & Schuster Building, Rockefeller Center, 1230 Avenue of the Americas, New York, New York 10020. Compilation copyright © 1991 by Lee Bennett Hopkins. Illustrations copyright © 1991 by Hilary Knight. All rights reserved including the right of reproduction in whole or in part in any form. SIMON & SCHUSTER BOOKS FOR YOUNG READERS is a trademark of Simon & Schuster. Designed by Sylvia Frezzolini. The text of this book is set in 12 point Diotima. The illustrations were done in watercolor, pen and ink, and colored pencil. Manufactured in Hong Kong

2 4 6 8 10 9 7 5 3 1

Library of Congress Cataloging-in-Publication Data: Happy birthday / compiled by Lee Bennett Hopkins; illustrated by Hilary Knight. Summary: A collection of poems all about birthdays. 1. Birthdays—Juvenile poetry. 2. Children's poetry, American. [1. Birthdays—Poetry. 2. American poetry—Collections.] I. Hopkins, Lee Bennett. II. Knight, Hilary, ill. PS595.B57H36 1991 811.008'033—dc20 90-10086 CIP AC   ISBN 0-689-83877-8 Revised Jacket Edition, 2000